This book belongs to

....

For Theo (even though he's a teenager now) P.B.

For the lovely and brilliant Sarah Malley G.P-R.

Diggory Digger
and the Dinosaurs
the

Peter Bently

Illustrated by **Guy Parker-Rees**

DEAN

When Builder Matilda went off for her tea
She said, "Can you finish this sandpit by three?"
"No problem!" said Diggory.
"Leave it to me!"

He swung down his scoop
with a WHIRR and a CLUNK,
Chomped at the ground
and bit out a chunk.

"Hey!" he declared.
"I've discovered a hole."
"It looks like a tunnel,"
said Morris the Mole.

"Come on!" said Diggory. "Hop in my cab.
Let's go exploring! Exploring is fab!"

Past tunnels and caverns as black as the night.

Then Diggory came to a stop with a shock.

"What's blocking the way? It's a great yellow rock!"

He bulldozed the boulder,
but just couldn't lift it.

He whacked and he walloped,
but nothing would shift it.

Then the boulder went GRUNT!
It **snorted** and **growled!**

It opened an eye!

And another!

And **HOWLED!**

Diggory cried, "That's no boulder before us!"

"No," squeaked the Mole. "It's a . . .

...Diggerosaurus!"

"I'll gobble you up!" roared the beast as it rose.
"You've woken me up from my million-year doze."

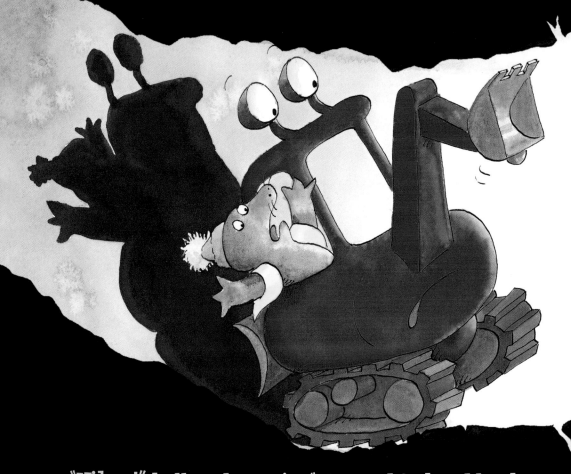

"Yikes!" hollered Morris. "We need to head back
Or we're both going to end up a dinosaur snack!
But how can we flee from a monster so big?"
"There's only one answer," said Diggory. "**Dig!**"

Down through the earth little Diggory chomped.
But hot on his heels the huge dinosaur stomped.

"Anywhere you can dig I can dig quicker,"
Cackled the beast with a sneer and a snicker.
Closer it came with its awesome great claws
And its awesome great teeth in its awesome great jaws.

"Help!" Morris howled as they dug round a bend.
"We're lost and it's catching us up. It's the end!"

"**Look,** here's a cave. What a great place to hide!"
Said Diggory, speedily sprinting inside.
He zipped out of sight and declared, "Safe at last."
As the **Diggerosaurus** went thundering past.

Then out of the darkness there came a loud GROAN.
"Oh dear," muttered Morris. "We're not on our own."
Morris and Diggory trembled with fright

as . . .

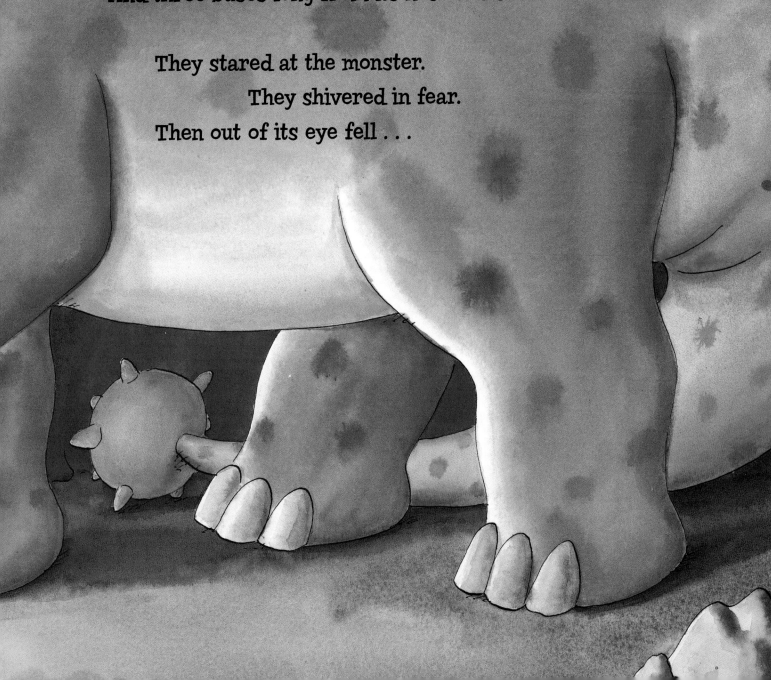

. . . a **BIGGEROSAURUS**

limped into the light.

It was **huge**. It was **vast**. It was wide as a whale
And three buses long from its nose to its tail.

They stared at the monster.
They shivered in fear.
Then out of its eye fell . . .

Diggory Digger looked closely
and saw
That something was stuck
in the dinosaur's paw.

The **BIGGEROSAURUS** gave a great moan
As Diggory plucked out a very sharp stone.

Diggory said, "That should stop all your pain."
"**Thanks!**" said the dinosaur.
"Thank you, again!"

He gave the two friends an enormous great grin,
then —

... the **Diggerosaurus** came galloping in!

"I've found you!" it snarled. "You've got nowhere to flee.
Who'll save you **now?**"

And a voice replied, "**ME!**"

The **BIGGEROSAURUS**, with fierce blazing eyes,
Boomed: "Pick on a digger that's more your **own size!**"

"ARRGGHH!"

roared the **Diggerosaurus** in dread,
As it turned on its tail and rapidly fled.

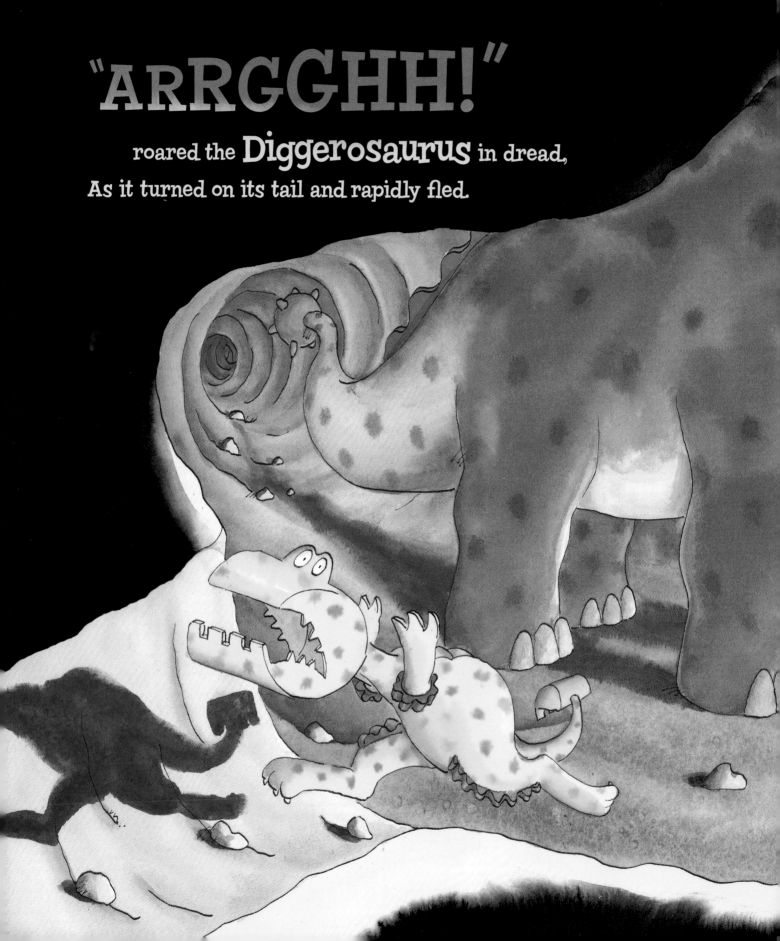

"And now," smiled the

BIGGEROSAURUS with glee,

"I'll show you the passageway home.

Follow me!"

Where the tunnel had been
there was nothing to see
When Builder Matilda
came back from her tea.

"There!" declared
Diggory,
      covered in grime.
"Another job finished
      exactly on time."

And the **Diggerosaurus**? He's digging away . . .

He caused a small earthquake in Paris today . . .

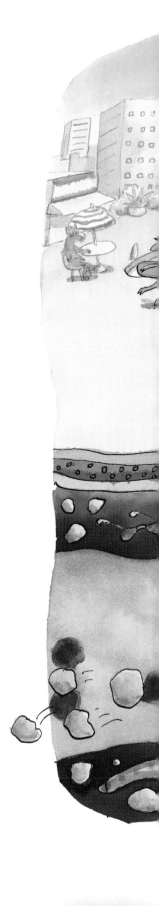

And startled some wombats near Sydney, Down Under.

Is he tunnelling right below YOUR house, I wonder?

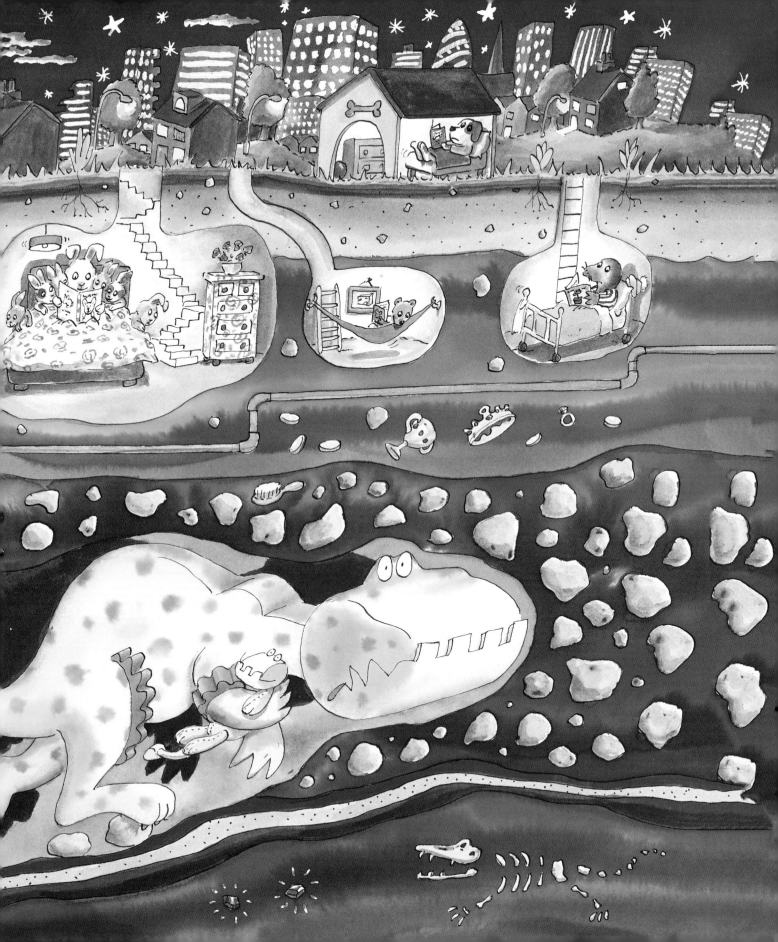

DEAN

First published in Great Britain 2013 by Egmont UK Limited
This edition published 2019 by Dean,
an imprint of Egmont UK Limited,
The Yellow Building, 1 Nicholas Road, London W11 4AN

www.egmont.co.uk

Text copyright © Peter Bently 2013
Illustrations copyright © Guy Parker-Rees 2013

The moral rights of the author and illustrator have been asserted.

ISBN 978 0 6035 7763 5
70746/1
Printed in Malaysia

A CIP catalogue record for this title is available from the British Library.

Stay safe online. Any website addresses listed in this book are correct at the time of going to print. However, Egmont is not responsible for content hosted by third parties. Please be aware that online content can be subject to change and websites can contain content that is unsuitable for children. We advise that all children are supervised when using the internet.

Egmont takes its responsibility to the planet and its inhabitants very seriously. We aim to use papers from well-managed forests run by responsible suppliers.

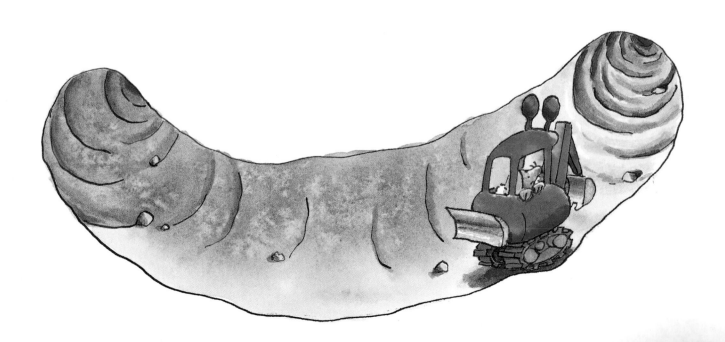